For Priyanka and Nikhil —S. M.

To Saurabh, Sanyukta, Papa, and Bhuaji —C. P. M.

Henry Holt and Company, *Publishers since 1866*
Henry Holt® is a registered trademark of Macmillan Publishing Group, LLC.
120 Broadway, New York, NY 10271
mackids.com

Library of Congress Cataloging-in-Publication Data is available.
ISBN 978-1-250-25746-8

Our books may be purchased in bulk for promotional, educational, or business use. Please contact your local
bookseller or the Macmillan Corporate and Premium Sales Department at (800) 221-7945 ext. 5442 or by email at
MacmillanSpecialMarkets@macmillan.com.
First Edition, 2021
The illustrations were rendered in pencil, ink, and watercolor, with a little digital magic.

Printed in China by RR Donnelley Asia Printing Solutions Ltd., Dongguan City, Guangdong Province
1 3 5 7 9 10 8 6 4 2

HAPPY DIWALI!

Written by
Sanyukta Mathur

Written and illustrated by
Courtney Pippin-Mathur

Christy Ottaviano Books

Henry Holt and Company · New York

Clean the house, everyone helps!

Let's hang up the lights so they shine nice and bright!

Draw rangolis to welcome our guests.

Hang decorations!

Gol gappas

Chana masala

Cook the food!

Sukhe aloo

Puffy puris!

Get dressed up in flowing silks and cottons with bright colors, shiny sequins, and threads that make beautiful designs.

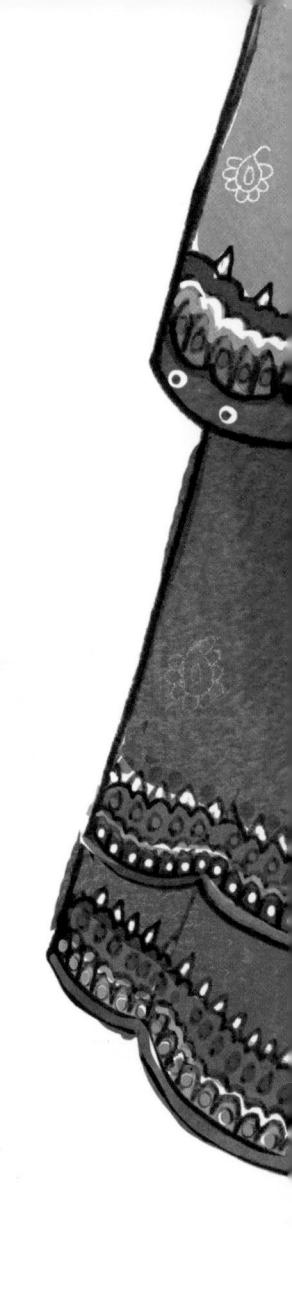

Welcome our friends and family!

Paint the diyas to hold the lights.

Perform the puja to
the goddess Lakshmi
for prosperity.

Listen to the stories of brave Lord Rama, devoted Laxman;
clever Hanuman, beautiful Sita; and evil King Ravana,
and of how the diyas
lit the path home.

Eat the food,

drink the mango lassi.

Gobble the mithai!

This is how we celebrate Diwali at our home in the U.S. How do you celebrate Diwali?

What is Diwali? Diwali (pronounced dee-vaa-lee, and also known as Deepavali) is the Hindu festival of lights. It is the celebration of good triumphing over evil, knowledge over ignorance, and light over darkness.

What are the Diwali traditions? Cleaning and decorating the house, wearing new clothes, and visiting family are important parts of the celebration, along with lights, diyas, rangolis, fireworks, sparklers, and delicious food—especially sweets! It is always celebrated in the autumn, but the date moves based on the lunar calendar. How it is celebrated varies according to regional and family traditions.

A Note from the Authors: Celebrating Diwali is one of my fondest memories of growing up in Delhi, India. My mother would cook for days, our home would be decorated with lights, we would get new clothes and money (if we were lucky) from visiting friends and family, we would see Ram Leela (street theater retelling the stories of Ramayana), and there would be fireworks at every home and neighborhood to delight all. When our family moved to the United States, we continued with our Diwali celebrations. Now, with my own family, I have tried to re-create some of the celebrations. Courtney and I hope you enjoy reading this book and learning about how our family celebrates Diwali in the U.S. —Sanyukta

I am hugely grateful to be part of a diverse and welcoming family who work hard to bring their traditions to the United States and pass them along to new generations. —Courtney

GLOSSARY:

 **Rangolis:** intricate designs made from colored powders, chalk, sand, or flowers

 **Diyas:** small oil lamps

 Lassi: a sweet or savory drink made with yogurt

 **Mithai:** sweets including but not limited to burfee, ladoo, and gulab jamun

 **Puja:** a prayer service to the gods and goddesses; Ganesh (god of good beginnings), Lakshmi (goddess of wealth and prosperity), and Saraswati (goddess of knowledge, art, music, learning, and wisdom) are just some of the important gods at Diwali

Here are some delicious recipes you can try for Diwali! Some of the recipes involve using the stove, so a grown-up will need to assist you.

SANYUKTA'S MANGO LASSI

There are many different variations of lassi, a northern Indian yogurt-based drink. Some people enjoy salty or sweet, and others prefer it with fruits. In our family, mango lassi is the favorite.

Ingredients:

- 1 cup plain milk yogurt
- 1 cup mango (canned Alphonso mango pulp or frozen or freshly cubed sweet mango)
- 1 cup ice
- 1 cup milk
- 2–4 tablespoons sugar (or to taste)
- 1 teaspoon freshly ground cardamom seeds

Instructions:

1. Combine yogurt, mango, and ice in a blender. If using fresh or frozen mangoes, puree them finely before adding to the yogurt mix (you don't want any pulpy bits).
2. Add milk (if the yogurt is very thick, adding milk as needed can make it lighter and easier to drink) and continue to blend.
3. Add sugar a tablespoon at a time, tasting as you go, and blend.
4. Pour mixture into a cup and sprinkle with cardamom. Enjoy!

PAPA'S SUKHE ALOO

Potatoes are prepared in many different ways in India. Here is a favorite from our father.

Ingredients:

- 1–2 tablespoons canola or vegetable oil
- 1–2 teaspoons cumin seeds
- 4 medium-sized potatoes, boiled, cooled, and cut into 1/4-inch chunks
- 1–2 teaspoons salt
- 1/2 teaspoon turmeric (optional)

Instructions:

1. Heat oil in a skillet over medium-high heat.
2. Add cumin seeds.
3. When the seeds start to sputter, add the potatoes.
4. Add salt (to taste) and turmeric, if using. Stir gently.
5. Let the potatoes cook till they are a little crispy on the edges. Yum!

BHUAJI'S PURIS

Puris are delicious unleavened fried bread.
Our kids devour these puris, made with our aunt's recipe.

Ingredients:

- 2 cups whole wheat flour
- 2/3 cup plus 1 teaspoon water
- 2 cups plus 1 teaspoon canola or vegetable oil, plus more as needed for greasing and deep-frying

Instructions:

1. Place the flour in a medium-sized bowl, then slowly stir in the water, stopping when the dough feels medium-hard (you may not need to use all the water).

2. Mix in 1 teaspoon of the oil.

3. Knead the dough for 3 to 4 minutes or until smooth. The dough should not stick to the bowl.

4. Divide the dough into 1- to 1-1/2-inch balls. There should be enough for 18 balls.

5. On a flat surface or cutting board, use a rolling pin to flatten each ball into a circle about 3 to 4 inches in diameter. If the dough sticks, grease the board lightly with oil. Place the rolled-out puris on a cookie sheet, in a single layer, as you go.

6. Heat the oil in a wok or deep-frying pan over medium heat. Don't let the oil get too hot. To test the temperature, place one puri in the oil and use a slotted spatula to press the puri lightly. If the puri comes up to the surface of the oil and starts to puff, your oil is ready to fry.

7. Fry one puri at a time, cook for 1 minute, flip over, and cook for 1 minute more.

8. Place the fried puris on a dish lined with paper towels to soak up the extra oil.

9. You can serve the puris right away or keep them for later.